The Candle Maker

Laura Thomas

The Candle Maker   Laura Thomas

ALL RIGHTS RESERVED

Publishers Note:

This is a work of fiction. All names, characters, places, and events are the work of the author's imagination. Any resemblance to real persons, places, or events is coincidental.

DWB PUBLISHING
CHILDReNS LINe
www.dwbchildrensline.com

Dedicated to my sons, Jameson and Jacob
Who inspire and amuse me every single day...

The Candle Maker   Laura Thomas

~ One ~

Benjamin Walker's teeth chattered uncontrollably. It was not from the bitter cold this snowy Christmas Eve—he was used to freezing under his thin jacket and flat cap. Today he was shivering out of fear—his biggest fear.

"Don't just stand there, Ben. Mother will skin you alive if you don't come home with her special Christmas candle. You don't really believe what folks say about the old candle maker, do you?"

Benjamin snorted at his younger brother. "Jimmy, you don't understand. When you're ten years old it will be *your* turn to buy the candle. Then you'll know how scary it really is."

Jimmy scuffed his boot on the snowy sidewalk and sighed. "I've got two whole years to wait. Besides, I won't be a big baby like you."

Benjamin shoved his brother's arm. He stared up at the candle maker's shop and took a deep breath. He didn't want to cross the road. Maybe his feet were frozen to the snow and that's why he couldn't move. Or maybe he was simply scared stiff.

Little Jimmy shifted from one foot to the other, trying his best to stay warm. Benjamin glanced down at their ragged clothes. They always wore hand-me-downs from their four older brothers. This evening they both had woolen scarves wrapped around their scrawny necks, knitted especially by Grandma Ethel. Even so, they were freezing cold and looked like pitiful beggars.

Suddenly, the first street lamp came alive. Benjamin loved to watch the lamp men. They made the old English streets look warm and cozy on dark afternoons. A horse and cart rushed past the boys, and they quickly jumped back. Slush covered their old boots and splashed up their trousers.

Benjamin shook himself and then stood tall. "Okay, Jimmy, it's time for me to go. You wait here. I'll only be five minutes. If I don't come back out..."

"What, Ben? What will I do if you don't come back out? Run home and tell Father?" Jimmy's eyes shone with tears.

"Yes. That's a good plan. You're a good little brother."

Benjamin grinned and tugged on Jimmy's cap before he turned to face his doom. The road was still bustling with shoppers, probably all buying last minute gifts for tomorrow. Benjamin sighed. What would it be like to have a pile of gifts to open on Christmas Day? He would only get one—if he were lucky. But now he had to buy his mother's candle. Looking both ways, he crossed the narrow street.

"Ben."

Benjamin stopped and spun around. "What?"

Jimmy waved. "I'll say a prayer for you."

Benjamin stared a bit longer than he needed to and froze for a moment. Would ever see his brother again? Finally, he waved back.

In front of the shop, Benjamin's stomach flip-flopped and he felt every heartbeat deep in his chest. His ears filled with rhythmical sounds of whooshing and pulsing.

With one foot on the stone step, Benjamin lifted his chilly hand and touched the doorknob. The other hand pushed his yo-yo deeper into his trouser pocket. It was his only toy, and he remembered what his older brother Charlie said last night. *"Don't let the old candle maker see your yo-yo, Benjamin. He takes yo-yo's from little boys and uses the strings for his candle wicks."*

"No way he's getting my yo-yo," Benjamin muttered into the frigid air. He felt brave for a short moment.

On the black, wooden door a big bunch of Christmas holly hung from a nail, and when Benjamin pushed hard, the sound of sleigh bells rang out. He entered and a sudden wave of heat washed over him, and he was warm for the first time all day.

The shop was larger than it appeared from the outside and had an old feeling. Maybe it was because the candle maker was old. Some said he was a hundred years old. Benjamin quickly glanced around. He was completely alone. Rows of candles in every color surrounded the place and Benjamin noticed their long wicks sticking out the ends. He felt for the yo-yo in his pocket, to be sure it was still safe.

Folks told Benjamin he was tall for a ten-year-old, but he felt like a puny cricket when he stood next to the high counters.

9

Maybe the whispers were true and the candle maker really was ten feet tall with the longest legs in the world.

"Yes? Can I help you?"

There he was, in the flesh—the candle maker. Benjamin was finally face-to-face with his biggest fear. In a split second Benjamin looked the old man up and down. He had white, stringy hair, and lots of it. A long hooked nose made him look like an eagle. His skin was so pale it was almost the color of his hair, and made his crooked teeth look extra yellow.

"Yes?" the old man croaked, a little more loudly this time.

Benjamin opened his mouth but no sound came out. His mind was fuzzy and no words were there.

The candle maker started to bend down toward Benjamin very slowly. When he was an arm's length away, Benjamin screamed. He couldn't help it. He turned and ran for the big door, yanked it open and darted outside as fast as his legs would carry him. The door slammed behind him but he didn't turn back. Benjamin's chest heaved as he ran across the road.

"You can't get me now, old candle maker. Can you?"

~ Two ~

"Chestnuts. Lovely hot chestnuts!"

Benjamin almost ran straight into the chestnut vendor in his rush to get away from the candle shop.

"Ben?" Jimmy stood with his hands on his skinny hips. "What's going on?"

"Run." Benjamin grabbed his little brother's arm on his way past.

The boys were both fast runners, and often raced each other through the cobbled streets of Bonnington. Benjamin even won first place for the dash in the school sports day. Today he was grateful for a light dusting of snow, which covered any icy patches and gave them a little traction.

"What happened?" Jimmy rasped between breaths.

Benjamin wasn't running full speed, so they were neck-and-neck as they raced down the street.

"I saw him." Benjamin tried not to sound afraid but his voice squeaked a little bit. "And he's as scary as they say."

Jimmy gasped, turned to make sure they weren't being followed, and then continued running alongside his brother.

"He won't come after us, silly. He's about a hundred years old." Benjamin panted in a slightly braver voice. "I want to go home, that's all."

"But what about Mother's candle?"

Benjamin bit his lip, and tasted blood as he pictured his mother's disappointed face. "I don't know."

Alongside them, the sight of blurring shops gradually changed to rows of cramped houses and Benjamin felt his heartbeat return to a normal rate when they slowed to a jog. They were nearly home.

"Who are you running from, little Walker boys?"

The biggest of a bunch of teenagers leaned against the wall at the end of an alley. The others snickered and one of them flicked ash from a cigarette, which nearly landed on Jimmy's sleeve.

"Keep going, Jimmy, we're almost home."

11

Benjamin dreaded passing that alley. The big boys thought they owned the village and always picked on the Walkers. Benjamin had four older brothers—Sam, William, Frank, and Charlie, who usually kept the troublemakers at bay but without their protection, he was always a little nervous.

One more corner and Benjamin caught sight of his house. It wasn't anything special in this plain, little village on the outskirts of London but it was home. Mother always kept it warm and cozy in the winter, and seeing as how his father was a chimney sweep, they had a good fire burning most days in the winter.

Benjamin slowed down. A curl of pale grey smoke drifted from their chimney into the darkening sky, and a light shone through drab curtains in the living room. Mother would be busy fixing something for tea, most likely. When he approached the black front door with the peeling paint, he heard the whistle of the teakettle.

Jimmy tugged at his brother's sleeve. "You know she's going to be really sad about the candle, don't you, Ben? She saves her sewing money for it especially. It's her only Christmas present."

Benjamin shrugged. "What was I supposed to do? Get kidnapped by the candle maker? I barely escaped with my life."

"Boys? Benjamin and Jimmy, is that you?" Mother's singsong voice rang out from the kitchen, and the brothers wrestled through the front door together.

The warmth felt so good, for a moment Benjamin forgot about the candle. Their tiny living room was decorated with colorful homemade paper chains, and the sad little Christmas tree in the corner seemed to be standing extra tall this Christmas Eve. The scent of pine needles in the air mixed with something delicious.

"Mmm. What's that lovely smell?" Jimmy rushed over to his mother and gave her a fierce hug.

She laughed and held his ruddy cheeks with both hands. "You are freezing, my boy. And that's the smell of Christmas."

"It's good enough to eat." Benjamin stomped a dusting of snow from his worn boots, and carefully avoided making eye con-

12

tact with his mother while he removed his cap.

"I made some hot apple cider with cinnamon and cloves, and everything." Her face beamed. "Dear Mrs. Worthington dropped over the ingredients this morning and said I should spoil my boys."

"I love Mrs. Worthington." Jimmy grinned.

While Jimmy shed his coat and cap, Benjamin stood awkwardly by the door.

"Are you okay?" His mother came over and touched his forehead. "I hope you're not getting sick on Christmas Eve, Ben."

"He didn't get your candle," Jimmy piped up from the kitchen.

Benjamin chanced a glance at his mother and watched her face fall. She wouldn't make a fuss or get angry—she wasn't like that. But when he saw a sheen of tears spring to her eyes, his chest hurt from the inside out. This was her tradition, the one thing she bought for herself at Christmas. Her precious red candle for the Christmas dinner table made her feel rich and proper, so she said.

"I'm sorry, Mother, really I am. It's just that the candle maker came toward me in his shop and I thought he was going to grab me, so I ran. I've heard about what happens to children who get caught by him."

Mrs. Walker knelt in front of her son and looked into his eyes. "Benjamin, I'm not angry about the candle. It's only a candle, and we'll still have a lovely dinner tomorrow. But I don't like you listening to silly rumors in the village. I hope you don't join in—you know what the Good Book says about taming the tongue. I've known the candle maker since I was a little girl, and he's a fine fellow. Have any of your brothers ever been hurt by him, or captured, or grabbed when they fetched my candle each year?"

"No." Benjamin fought back tears.

"Do you really think I would ever send you anywhere dangerous for a little candle?"

"No." Benjamin stood to his full height and pulled the cap back onto his head. "I'm not afraid, Mother. I'm going back right now to get your red candle. Christmas dinner won't be the same without it. I'll hurry."

Mrs. Walker chewed her lip and pulled the dingy lace curtain to one side as she peered into the street. "I don't know, son. It's getting pretty dark out there now, and I don't like you going into the village center on your own. Don't worry about my candle. Stay in where it's warm and I'll get you a nice mug of hot apple cider."

"I *have* to go. Please, let me do this for you. Charlie and the others will never let me live it down if they find out I was scared." He shot a warning look to Jimmy.

"Okay then. But wait for Charlie to come home and he'll run over with you. The boys are all due back any minute."

"Thanks, Mother. I'll wait outside for Charlie." Benjamin hurried out the front door before his mother could argue, and closed it behind him.

It was certainly dark now, and huge snowflakes fell in slow motion, some even caught on his eyelashes. He pulled his cap down tighter and looked both ways along the dimly lit street. All the houses were the same, and their front doors were right on the pavement. No yards or gardens in this area of the village. Benjamin secretly wished he had a lovely big house with a gigantic yard to play in.

He shook his head and stopped daydreaming. He had a mission, and he had no intention of waiting around for his brother.

He had to do this alone.

~ Three ~

Benjamin clutched his threadbare jacket tightly around his skinny waist. He put his head down and started the journey back to Main Street and the candle maker. It was best not to run full speed, since visibility wasn't perfect this late in the day, and the last thing he wanted to do was fall down and twist an ankle.

The street had that strange silence about it tonight—it was as if the layer of snow muted every single noise. Most families were safe and warm enjoying their Christmas Eve supper together, maybe singing or playing games, or reading the Christmas story from the Bible.

Benjamin smiled when he thought of his own family. Father would be home soon after a hard day cleaning chimneys. The soot blackened his skin, and his cough was deep and dry but he enjoyed his work. He knew exactly what happened when Father came home. The kiss he planted on Mother's cheek always left a sooty, black mark but Mother laughed and slapped at him, giggling like a schoolgirl. They were poor but happy. Father said they were blessed indeed.

Glancing through the windows as he passed by, Benjamin wished he were an only child. He would so enjoy his parents' undivided attention and all the presents for him alone. He wrinkled his nose. Who was he trying to kid? He loved his big brothers, even when they wrestled him too hard and teased him to death. Plus little Jimmy was a good boy—at least there was one brother he could boss around.

The row of huddled houses came to an end and Benjamin hesitated. He could continue along the lamp lit street, or run through the dark alley and shave off a chunk of time. How much longer would the candle store stay open? Without thinking about it too deeply, he decided to take the alley.

Benjamin trod carefully and dodged various obstacles that littered the long path. He started to whistle a carol. Whistling usually calmed him, plus it would let anyone know he was walking this way, and hopefully avoid a collision. When he brushed his hand along the side of the brick wall, its roughness caught on his

15

woolen, fingerless gloves. Now he could barely feel his exposed fingertips. He almost bumped into a steel garbage bin, and carefully stepped around it. Then he heard a noise.

Benjamin stopped in his tracks and stood as still as a statue. A low, throaty sound came from the ground. Not a growl exactly, but it sounded like an animal. He tentatively stretched his foot to the side where the sound seemed to be coming from, and sure enough, a solid warm shape huddled up against the garbage bin.

Curious, Benjamin slid the bin along the wall until the shape was partially visible in the silver moonlight.

"You're a dog."

Delighted, but cautious in case the animal was hurt or vicious, Benjamin gently placed his hand on the dog's head.

"There, boy, I'm not gonna hurt you, I love dogs. You're all right. I'm a friend."

For a minute or so, he continued stroking the dog's matted fur. The poor thing was shaking either from fear or the biting cold air, or maybe a bit of both. Benjamin's eyes adjusted to the dark, and he noticed the animal was mostly tan with a white patch over one eye—definitely an English bulldog. Benjamin had seen the breed before and recognized the wrinkly face and broad chest, only this one looked quite skinny and tired. Benjamin's heart broke when he felt the outline of ribs and bones too clearly.

"What happened to you, boy? Are you lost? Did you get thrown out?"

Benjamin always wanted a dog of his own, but his parents insisted it would be too much of an expense. Luckily, his brother Charlie loved animals and was smart, so he worked alongside the country vet on weekends, and occasionally even brought a dog home to visit. His parents didn't seem to mind as long as they didn't have to feed it.

"I'm going to call you Butch." Benjamin tickled the dog's ears. "How do you like that?"

Butch seemed calm, so Benjamin decided to scout around for some food. "There must be some scraps around here somewhere." Only a couple of empty cans littered the ground, so Benjamin decided to delve into the large garbage bin.

"My mother would tan my hide if she knew I was doing this, Butch. It'll be our little secret, okay?" He scrunched up his face and felt around for something edible. "Oh yuck. This does not feel good. I have some potato peelings..." He dropped a handful on the dirt next to the dog. "And, oh, I think I've found something a little more tasty—a piece of meat. It's a bit squishy and I can't promise what sort of meat it is, but I think you'll like it."

Sure enough, Butch sniffed the hunk of food and gobbled it down in seconds, and then turned to the potato peelings and swallowed them, too.

"You must have been starving, boy. When was the last time you ate something?"

The poor dog looked up with sad, chocolate brown eyes and let out a sorrowful sigh before rolling onto his back. He looked so pitiful, Benjamin took a few minutes to give him a belly rub and show him some love.

"There you go, Butch. Is that better?"

Suddenly, the dog jumped to his feet.

"What is it?" Benjamin turned to look down the dark alley and froze.

Butch started a low, menacing growl, directed further down the path. Benjamin squinted but couldn't see anyone there.

"It's okay, boy, there's no one here but you and me. No need to be afraid." Even as he spoke the words, his heart beat faster. He strained his ears to hear something other than the growling, and recognized the sound of muffled footsteps—several sets of them, shuffling in his direction from the opposite end of the alley.

"I should have listened to Mother. I should have waited for Charlie. But I'm tired of being so afraid today." First, it was the candle maker, and then the bullies, and now the strange noises in the darkness. It was probably a family out for a Christmas Eve stroll, or it may be the local policeman making his rounds. Only he was pretty sure there were at least four sets of footsteps, and they were getting closer every second. Low voices carried on the night air, and Benjamin had to make a quick decision.

He could run back home and disappoint his mother for the

second time, or face his fears in the alley and then again at the candle store. He stood squarely next to his new growling friend and waited to see what would become of him.

~ Four ~

"Well, well, well. If it isn't one of the little Walker boys."

Benjamin's heart sank when the figures before him brightened in the moonlight. It was the gang of four teenaged bullies who teased him earlier when he was with Jimmy. They were always picking on one of the younger children in the neighborhood. They looked even taller close up, and they didn't seem to be in a very festive mood. Clearly, they weren't out enjoying a Christmas Eve stroll.

"Got a new friend there, have we?" The tallest one pointed at the dog.

"I-I found him here," Benjamin stammered, "and he was hungry and cold. I think he's lost."

"Poor puppy. My heart bleeds. Well guess what? I'm hungry and cold, too."

The other three laughed.

"Good one, Smith." A shorter, stocky boy pointed at Benjamin. "Maybe young Walker will feed you."

Benjamin wanted to run back home the way he came, but his legs felt like cement. He glanced down at the dog, who had somehow found the energy to stand and look mean.

"Good boy," he whispered.

"What did you say?" The boy named Smith snarled. "What are you whispering to that animal? I know he's not yours. I've seen him down here before. He's a stray and he'll probably be dead from the cold by the New Year."

"No he won't." Benjamin folded his arms over his chest. "I'll see to that."

Smith raised one brow and tapped his finger on his pointed chin. "Is that right, Walker?"

Benjamin gulped. "Look, what do you want? I need to run an errand and I'm late."

Smith snickered. "It's Christmas, and you haven't given me my present yet." Benjamin's mouth dropped open. "That's okay, I understand. You're dirt poor."

The group agreed loudly and Benjamin's cheeks flushed.

19

"Tell you what, you can give me the money you have in your pocket, and we'll call it even. Okay?"

Benjamin thrust both hands in his pockets. His yo-yo was still in one, and the sixpence for his mother's candle was in the other. There was no way these bullies were getting either.

"Don't try to pretend you haven't got anything. If you're running an errand, there's bound to be money involved."

Benjamin shivered, and wished his big brothers would come along to sort this mess out.

"Come on then, time's a-wasting." Smith reached out and grabbed Benjamin's cap clean off his head. The gang laughed, but a menacing sound followed. The bulldog stood protectively in front of Benjamin and barked, baring his sharp teeth.

One of the boys jumped back. "Hey, we shouldn't get this one mad. Look at his teeth. Let's leave it and go."

Another deep growl from the bulldog echoed all the way down the alley.

"He's all bark. Look how scrawny he is." Smith pointed to Butch's ribs. "Come on, Walker, I'm in a hurry here, and your mutt's getting impatient."

"No." Benjamin felt like jelly inside, but jutted his chin and stood next to the dog.

Smith bent down and picked up a stone covered in snow. "Let's see how brave your dog is then, shall we?" He pulled back his arm and the stone flew through the air.

Benjamin dove in front of the dog, and covered his head with his right arm. He landed on the frozen ground with a thud, but was relieved that his shoulder had taken the hit, and Butch was safe. He didn't move until he felt something warm tickling his neck. Butch licked his thanks.

"Hey, boy, we're okay."

"Oh, how sweet." Smith stood right above Benjamin, his face quivering with anger. "Nobody gets in my way, Walker. Especially a little kid like you."

Butch growled louder than before, and the boys all inched back slightly.

"You better call your scrawny dog away, otherwise he'll

see the bottom of my boot." Smith playfully slapped another lad on the back and they all laughed. "What do you think, boys, shall we see if this bulldog is as tough as he thinks he is?"

"Do it," the stocky one replied. "He doesn't look like he's got the strength to fight a kitten."

Benjamin's pulse quickened and he knew he had to do something to protect Butch. With a quick prayer for courage, he took one step forward until he was almost toe-to-toe with Smith.

"Your problem isn't with the dog, it's with me. But there's no way I'm giving in to a bully and handing over my mother's money. Why don't you let me pass? Don't you have any Christmas cheer at all?"

"No. None. But I might cheer up if I had your cash. This is your last chance, boy. Hand over your money."

Even though Benjamin was freezing cold, a trickle of sweat slid down the side of his face, and he braced himself for whatever might happen next. With five brothers, fighting was a way of life, but these boys wouldn't let him off easily.

"If you want my money, you'll have to take it."

"Fine, then I'll teach you a lesson and grab it myself—"

Before the bullies had chance to lay a finger on Benjamin, the bulldog lunged in their direction and gripped onto Smith's lanky arm. The boy screeched.

"Get your crazy dog off me!" Smith's face turned bright red, and a purple vein rose on his forehead. He flung the animal against the wall causing it to howl, and then turned to see his friends had already deserted him. "Next time, Walker."

Smith scurried after his friends and out of sight.

Benjamin could hear his own panting breath. *That was close.* He picked up his old cap from the ground and dusted it off before planting it firmly back on his head.

"Butch? Where are you, my good, brave dog? Here, boy." The moon shifted and the light was poor. The dog must have limped away into the shadows to lick his wounds.

"It's me, boy." Benjamin frantically kicked the cans out of the way and made his way down the alley as he searched for Butch. He checked behind every bin and frozen shrub that poked from the brick walls. Could the injured dog have run back the way Benjamin came in? Because now he was nowhere to be seen.

"Butch?" Benjamin's heart sank and his shoulders slumped. He had to get to the candle shop right away. He was already running late.

He bit the side of his cheek to stop any tears from falling. The poor, brave dog would be left all alone again on a freezing Christmas Eve.

~ Five ~

Benjamin took one last look down the alley to make sure the dog wasn't there, and then turned onto the street. He pulled up the collar of his jacket and thrust both hands deep into his pockets. The evening was getting colder and a brisk wind picked up.

"Poor Butch." He closed his eyes for a moment. "Dear God, please look after my new friend. And help him find somewhere to take cover this Christmas Eve. Amen."

His footsteps crunched in the snow as he made his way down the familiar road and passed a smattering of shops. The lights still glowed in most of the windows, and he prayed the candle maker's shop would still be open. Butch was heavy on Benjamin's mind, and while he hurried along the cobbled street, he quickly checked behind any object large enough to hide a dog.

"Butch. Here, boy, it's me." His cries disappeared into the snowy night.

Everyone looked to be in a rush when Benjamin approached Main Street. Last minute shoppers clutched parcels wrapped in brown paper and tied with string. Would he even get his very own Christmas present this year? Sometimes the boys had to share a gift.

"Butch would have been a perfect Christmas present for me."

Suddenly, a tall woman ran right in front of him in an attempt to avoid a horse and carriage, which was going way too fast along the pitted road.

"Sorry, son—oh, Benjamin Walker, is that you?"

Benjamin pulled his cap back and recognized his school-teacher, Miss Pritchard.

"Oh, hello Miss Pritchard. You nearly ran me over there, Miss."

The friendly teacher fussed and made sure Benjamin was all right. "Why, Benjamin, you look awfully sad and lonely considering it's Christmas Eve. Whatever are you doing out here by yourself? You should be indoors, cozy with your family."

Benjamin sighed. "I'm not having a good day, Miss Pritchard. I let my mother down because I believed some rumors, and then I let a dog down. It's a long story."

His teacher shivered and pulled her woolen shawl tightly around her shoulders. "Rumors are a nasty business. Best not to take part. But you're a good boy with a good heart. I know you'll make it right. You send my regards to your family."

"Thanks, Miss Pritchard."

"Oh, and Benjamin."

"Yes, Miss?" Benjamin looked into the kind eyes of the lady smiling before him.

"I hope you have the best Christmas ever."

Benjamin shrugged. "I doubt it. But thanks. And Merry Christmas to you, too."

He watched Miss Pritchard bustle down the road. He never imagined she had a life outside school. A dog barked and Benjamin swung around to see where the noise was coming from. He groaned when he saw a golden lab terrorizing a fat ginger cat.

"Definitely not Butch." With a heavy heart and sagging shoulders, he walked on at a steady pace.

Benjamin was so worried about Butch, and so sorry for letting his mother down, he barely gave the candle maker a thought. But when he stood opposite the candle shop in the exact same spot as he had earlier that afternoon, fear strangled his throat and he found it difficult to breathe. He gasped when he spotted the old man dangling his long arms over a display in the window.

The little panes of glass were starting to fill with snow, although it was clear what was happening inside, even from a distance.

"Wow, it's true."

Benjamin heard rumors that the candle maker would light a candle in his window display in the evening, and then secretly peer out into the village, searching for young children. Sure enough, there he was. He held a lit candle and pressed his long, crooked nose against the pane of glass, obviously looking for the next victim.

Benjamin's heart almost stopped when the candle maker's

gaze met his own. Even from across the street, he could feel the ancient eyes piercing the darkness.

"He must recognize me from before, and now he wants to catch me because I escaped. Maybe he has a cage full of children in the storeroom. They must have been there for years. Everyone in school says so."

He wasn't actually sure what the old man did with the children he captured, but it didn't really matter. The candle maker beckoned him with a gnarly finger, and at that moment, the red Christmas candle for his mother was the only thing that mattered. He was a disappointment to Butch and he would not be a disappointment to his mother.

"What if I never come out alive? Mother has to know I at least tried to get her candle." In a moment of pure genius, he pulled his cap from his head and hung it on the black iron railing, right opposite the store.

Instantly, his head felt chilly, but he stood tall and took his first step. He had no choice but to cross the snow-covered road and enter the dreaded lair of the scariest man in the village.

~ Six ~

Benjamin put one shaky hand on the doorknob. He gazed back across the street at his sorry excuse for a cap, which dangled limply on the railing. With a deep breath, he pushed the heavy door open once more and found himself back in his worst night-mare—the candle maker's shop.

His cheeks stung after being out in the chilly night, but the warmth of the room felt wonderful.

"Be right with you, son. I think you forgot your candle." The croaky voice came from the window display, and Benjamin spotted the old man bent over fiddling with something.

He took the opportunity to look around again. On closer in-spection, there were more than just candles for sale. Next to the till, he saw two long shelves filled with jars of candy. Peppermint sticks, licorice, golden toffee, and candy canes were lavishly dis-played before him. Sherbet lemons, aniseed twists, and striped peppermint humbugs beckoned from the row below. He breathed in and inhaled a wonderful mix of vanilla, cinnamon, and caramel. It smelled heavenly.

"How did I miss this before?"

"What's that?" The old man appeared on the other side of the counter, one hand cupped around his ear. "A bit hard of hear-ing, I'm afraid."

Benjamin shrugged. "Oh, nothing. I didn't know you sold sweets in here, that's all."

"Oh, yes. I always have a supply of treats here. Although not many youngsters come in these days."

Benjamin shuffled his feet. "So, I've come in for my moth-er's red Christmas candle." He placed the coin on the counter.

"Of course you have. I've been waiting for one of Mrs. Walker's boys to collect her usual red one." The candle maker slowly bent down to a shelf under the counter, grimacing on his way back up. "These poor old bones. You took off pretty quickly before. I didn't even get chance to offer you a candy cane. Would you like one, son?"

Benjamin's stomach gurgled a reply and the old man smiled. His face lit up, and kind wrinkles made his ancient eyes laugh. Suddenly, he didn't look very scary. In fact, he appeared quite jolly. He held the candy cane jar with an unsteady hand, and Benjamin slid one out and popped it in his pocket for later.

"Come on now, son, you really should take one for each of your brothers. It is Christmas after all."

"Really?" Benjamin's eyebrows shot up, but he remembered his manners. "Thank you, sir." He took a handful and grinned. He bit his lip and squinted up at the old man. "Excuse me for asking, but what do you do with all the children?"

"What's that?" The candle maker carefully wrapped the long, red candle in brown paper, and set it on the counter.

Benjamin's cheeks burned but he desperately needed to know. "The children. Where are they? The ones you capture."

A confused look passed over the old man's face and his bushy white eyebrows met in the middle.

Benjamin held his breath and clung on tightly to the yo-yo in his pocket. He was ready to face the truth and maybe even join the other captives. But instead of showing rage or evil, the candle maker started laughing. Not just a giggle, and not a frightening laugh, but a deep, belly laugh, which caused his whole face to scrunch up and turn quite pink. Benjamin crinkled his nose and shrugged, but couldn't help joining in.

Finally, the candle maker controlled himself enough to perch on a wooden stool and speak. He wiped tears from his eyes with a large, cotton handkerchief.

"That would explain why my sweets don't sell very quickly. Are those silly rumors really still flying around school, son? I can hardly believe it. I have been the talk of the village for so many years—only for the children, you understand. The grown-ups know better. Do tell me what they are saying these days, won't you?"

Benjamin's shoulders relaxed as he jumped up onto a matching stool and leaned against the counter.

"Are you sure you want to know, sir?"

"Positive."

"Most of the big kids have stories about you chasing them. Some say you capture the little ones and keep them locked up.

And then you use them as slaves to make your candles." He touched his yo-yo. "And you use their yo-yo strings for candle wicks."

At that, the old man started laughing again, until a fit of coughing forced him to stop.

"Is that right? Well, well…"

Benjamin cleared his throat. "And the other thing is the window candle. They say lately you peer through your window at dusk in the hopes of catching a child to do your work." He grinned. "I'm pretty sure now that's not right, but can I ask why you do that every evening? Are you looking for someone?"

The old man's face drooped and he slid from the stool. "As a matter of fact, I am looking for someone. Wait here for a minute."

Benjamin watched him slowly shuffle around the counter. How foolish he had been to believe the rumors all this time. The poor, old man couldn't run after anyone even if he wanted to. Mother was right. Words could be dangerous, and people should learn to tame their tongues. This gentleman was good and kind, and seemed rather lonely.

When the candle maker returned, he held a framed picture.

"What's this?" Benjamin took it from the shaky hand.

"This is who I look for every evening, son. This is who I wait for each night."

Benjamin gasped. "Butch?"

~ Seven ~

"That's my bulldog, Henry." The candle maker sighed. "I've had him for years, but one day a few months back, he disappeared. It was mighty strange. Of course, he may not still be alive but I have to believe he's out there somewhere, and perhaps one day he'll see the candle glowing in the window and come back home."

Benjamin couldn't speak. He studied the beautiful drawing in his hand. It was colored and full of detail, a real work of art. And one thing was for sure—it was Butch.

"Mister, I think I've seen him."

"What's that?" The old man leaned closer.

"Your bulldog, your Henry. I think he's my Butch."

The candle maker squinted. "Start at the beginning, son. Come to think of it, I don't even know your name. Which of the Walker boys are you?"

"I'm Benjamin—number five out of six."

"Okay, Benjamin, carry on."

"Tonight, on my way here, I came across this dog in the alley close to my house. I swear it's the same dog. That patch over his eye is unusual, and he had the same rusty colorings and everything. Only, he looked thinner." He gazed up into the candle maker's watery eyes. "And sadder."

"Oh, my." The old man covered his trembling mouth with one hand. "I knew he was out there somewhere. I don't have the legs to search very far. Why hasn't he come home? He may not be the smartest dog on the block but he was always faithful."

Benjamin jumped down from the stool and picked up his mother's candle from the counter. "We should take one last look. He can't have gone far. He may be injured..."

"What makes you say that, son?"

Benjamin looked down at his battered old boots. "Butch, I mean Henry, protected me when a gang of bullies tried to take my candle money back in the alley. I've always wanted a dog of my own, but Mother says no. But if I *did* ever have one, I would want him to be exactly like Henry. He's a very good dog."

"Yes, yes he is."

"Those boys were mean, and I think Henry may have been limping when he ran off. I tried to find him but couldn't. I had to get here in a hurry before you shut the shop."

"Oh, I'm in no rush to close. I've nothing to go hurrying home for really, now that Henry's not there. Poor old boy." The candle maker shrugged.

"But what about your family? Don't you need to get ready for Christmas?"

"There's only me, son. My darling wife passed away some years back, and we were never blessed with children of our own. This little shop is my family. It's my customers who make me feel part of this village."

Benjamin whistled through his teeth. "Oh. My little house is always so busy with the eight of us, I can't even imagine being on my own." He patted the candle maker's arm. "Come on, let's go find Henry."

"That's very sweet of you, but I'm afraid I'm not as spritely as I used to be. It's these poor old bones, they don't do well in the cold."

"Then I'll go by myself. I can't stand the thought of you being alone at Christmas, especially when I know your dog is alone, too. It's wrong." He picked up the wrapped candle and started toward the door.

"Son, wait. I'm very touched by your kindness but your mother will be worried if you're not home right away. Besides, it's Christmas Eve, and I'm sure there are a hundred other things you'd rather do than look for my Henry."

Benjamin shook his head. "Nope. Nothing I would rather do than find Henry, I promise. He's a special dog. If it makes you happy, I'll run home first and give Mother my candle, and tell her where I'm going. She'll probably send one of my big brothers with me, so I'll be fine." He opened the door and a gust of cold air hit him in the face. "I'll be back later—keep the candle burning."

The old candle maker waved, and a tear slid down his weathered cheek. "Oh I will, don't you worry. God bless you, Benjamin Walker."

~ Eight ~

Shivering in the falling flakes, Benjamin stuffed his mother's candle safely inside his jacket, and jogged across the street. He grabbed his cap from the railing—it was covered in snow, but a good shake shed the worst of it. He pulled it down over his head, and then spun around and took one last look at the candle store.

The candle maker leaned across the window display and waved the picture of Henry above his head. Benjamin waved back and then headed for home. He put his head down and ran as fast as he could. The candle dug into his stomach a little, but he couldn't bring himself to slow down. *I've made things right with Mother, and now I have to make things right with the bulldog and my new friend, the old candle maker.*

The streets were quiet now, and Benjamin smiled when the sound of carolers drifted on the air. He skidded to a stop at the entrance of the alley. He could sprint the long way around, which was probably safer.

"Tick-tock." Benjamin chose the alley. The carolers were no longer audible, and the quiet was eerie. He shivered and trudged along the dimly lit path. "At least I'll hear Smith and the gang if they come along with their noisy boots."

The silence stretched all the way along the alley. Benjamin could only hear the pad and crunch of his own footsteps in the snow until he passed the final rubbish bin near the end.

A single sound split the silence.

Benjamin stopped. He was so close to his house now, he wanted to start running again, but he was drawn to the bin. He stood perfectly still, straining his ears for another sound.

This time it was a sigh—a sad sigh, followed by a gentle bark.

"Butch? I mean *Henry*, is that you?" He tugged the heavy rubbish bin out of the way, and there was the bulldog, his big wrinkly head resting on his front paws.

"Henry." Benjamin dropped to his knees and buried his head in the dog's fur. Henry made a moaning sound, and Benjamin pulled back. "Are you hurt, boy?" He carefully ran his hands

31

down the dog's back and front legs, the way he had seen his brother Charlie check for injuries on animals. When he touched the right back leg, Henry let out a yelp.

"You have a nasty cut there, haven't you?" Benjamin could see it was injured but it didn't appear to be broken. "I'll be right back, Henry. I'm going to fetch help, okay?"

Henry's droopy, chocolate brown eyes closed and he lay his head back down on his paws.

Benjamin pulled out the candle and quickly unbuttoned his jacket. He peeled it off, and draped it tenderly over Henry's trembling body. "You need this more than I do, boy. I have to get this candle to my mother, but I'll be back."

He gave Henry's ears one last rub, and ran full speed all the way home.

"Benjamin, where on earth is your coat?" Mrs. Walker stood at the front door, her hands planted firmly on her hips. "And where have you been? I thought you were waiting for Charlie to go with you to the candle maker's? I've been worried sick."

Benjamin stomped the worst of the snow from his boots and hurried in through the door. "I'm sorry, Mother. But I have your special candle."

Mrs. Walker smiled and dimples appeared in her cheeks. "Thank you, son. You know this means the world to me." She brushed giant snowflakes from the shoulders of his patched sweater and gave him a warm hug. "But where is your coat? Surely you didn't lose it?"

Benjamin caught his breath and put his hand in his trouser pockets. The candy canes were still there.

"It's a long story, Mother, and I'm in a desperate hurry."

"You're home now, so come on over by the fire. Jimmy, will you fetch a nice mug of hot apple cider for our Benjamin, please?"

Jimmy jumped up from his game of jacks and headed for the kitchen. "Don't start the long story without me."

"I have to go back out, Mother," Benjamin explained. "And I was hoping you would come with me, Charlie." He looked over

32

at his big brother, who sat right next to the fire.

"Out where?" Charlie asked, rubbing his hands together. "I'm only just getting warm after being outside all day long."

"What's all this?" Mr. Walker plodded down the narrow stairs and stood among his sons.

"Oh, hello Father. Merry Christmas." Benjamin grinned sheepishly.

Mr. Walker was always exhausted after a day sweeping chimneys, and Benjamin hated to ask his family to give up their Christmas Eve, but there was a dog's life and an old man's happiness at stake.

"This is urgent, everyone." Benjamin took a deep breath. "I wanted to get Mother's candle, and I needed to do it all by myself. On my way, I met a stray dog, and that dog protected me from a gang of bullies in the alley."

"Smith?" Charlie asked.

Benjamin nodded.

"The dog got injured and ran away, so I rushed on to the candle shop." He looked at his four big brothers. "The old man's not mean at all, and he doesn't capture children and use their yo-yo strings for candle wicks."

Mr. Walker stifled a chuckle. "Benjamin, you mustn't believe everything you hear, son. Especially from your older brothers." He gave them a stern glare.

"I know that now, and look, he gave me a candy cane for each of us boys." He handed them out to much whooping and celebration. Every boy looked at his candy as if it were precious treasure.

Benjamin shrugged. "The kids at school tell the mean stories about him, too. I should never have listened. I know that now. We have to be very careful with our words." He glanced at his mother. "Anyway, the candle maker is really very friendly, but he's also very lonely. His dog ran away a few months ago, and he's been waiting for him to come home ever since."

Jimmy gasped. "Is it the stray you met, Ben? Is that the candle maker's dog?"

"Good guess, Jimmy. And I found him again on my way

home, right in the alley where I met him in the first place."

Jimmy pumped a fist in the air. "Good find, Ben. But where is he now?"

"He's injured from our run-in with Smith. I think his leg is hurt and he can't walk. That's where my coat is." He grimaced. "Sorry, Mother."

Mrs. Walker ruffled his hair.

Charlie grabbed a scarf and hat from the coat stand. "Come on, Ben. Show me where this dog is, and we'll carry him home. Mother, Father, is that okay? Just for tonight?"

Before his parents could answer, Benjamin blurted out, "No."

"What's wrong?" Charlie asked, giving his brother a shove. "Do you want us to help this dog or not?"

"Yes, of course." Benjamin looked around at his family. Most of the time he hated being the second-to-youngest in a big, noisy family. He wished they were rich and he wished his father didn't have to sweep chimneys for a living. He hated coal dust. But he was loved in a house full of life and laughter, and he dreaded the thought of ever being lonely.

"We need to get Henry back to his master. We need to get him home for Christmas."

~ Nine ~

Mrs. Walker sniffled. "That's very sweet of you, Benjamin. But how will you carry the dog all that way? Is he very big?"

Benjamin grinned. "Yeah, he's an English bulldog but I have it all figured it out."

"Really? What's your plan, son?" Mr. Walker perched on the stairs.

"Charlie will come with me to help lift Henry and make sure he's okay, and we can take him on Jimmy's red wagon. You don't mind, do you, Jimmy?"

The older boys sat back down to finish their card game, but Jimmy picked up his little cap. "You can borrow my wagon, but only if I can come, too. Mother, can I, please?"

Mr. Walker laughed and put an arm around his wife. "I'll go with them, dear. I know you'll worry if they're out there in the snow. Let's make the old man's Christmas special. It's the right thing to do. But make sure there's plenty of that hot apple cider for us when we come home."

Mrs. Walker kissed her husband's cheek, and then pecked Benjamin's, Charlie's, and Jimmy's before ushering them out of the house. She handed Benjamin one of his brother's jackets. "Oh, and Ben, be sure to invite the candle maker for Christmas dinner tomorrow, if he hasn't any other plans."

"You're the best mother ever."

Benjamin and his brothers dragged the wagon down the snowy street.

"Come on, I hope Henry is still in the alley."

Mr. Walker put a gloved hand on Benjamin's shoulder. "It sounds like he wouldn't be able to go very far on his own, even if he wanted to."

"Yeah. I'm afraid you're right."

A few minutes later, Benjamin stood at the entrance to the alley with Charlie, Jimmy, and their father.

Benjamin put one hand in the air. "Let me go first. Henry may get scared if we all arrive together. He knows I won't hurt him."

35

"Hurry then." Charlie clutched his sack of vet supplies.

Benjamin disappeared into the darkness, feeling a lot braver than before. "Henry, it's me. I've come back to help you, boy." He reached the rubbish bin, and dropped to the ground.

"Henry?" He touched the coat he had left on the dog. It lay in the dirt, discarded in a heap—with no Henry underneath.

"Oh no. Henry?" Benjamin jumped up and his family joined him.

"Where could he have gone?" Jimmy grabbed Benjamin's old coat from the ground. "Oh, there's blood on your coat, Ben. Yuck."

Mr. Walker took the coat, rolled it up, and tucked it under his arm. "Don't you worry about that, young Jimmy. Let's focus on the dog, he must be close by."

Charlie patted Benjamin's back. "The good news is, if he can walk then his leg is not too badly injured. Right?"

"I suppose so. But he'll be cold, and he thinks I left him alone again. We simply have to find him." Benjamin led the way slowly down the alley, while all of them called softly for the dog.

"The full moon is a big help, that's for sure." Mr. Walker looked up into the sky. "You can't usually see your hand in front of your face down here."

"Wait. Ben, look over there." Jimmy pointed toward a shadowy object at the end of the alley.

"Henry?" Benjamin sprinted down the lane and collapsed on the snow next to the dog. "Quickly, Jimmy, bring the wagon. Charlie, he's shaking really badly. Come and take a look at his leg."

Charlie talked in a soothing tone while he carefully felt Henry's limbs. "It's definitely not broken, but I'll wrap this nasty gash. Father, could you take out the bandage from my sack, please? Ben, you keep him calm while I work."

"What about me?" Jimmy pouted.

Mr. Walker tugged at Jimmy's cap. "You clear the wagon of any snow and use this coat of Ben's to make a nice blanket."

Jimmy beamed.

They worked together quickly, and soon the Walkers lay

36

Henry on the makeshift bed, which was now a considerable weight. They took turns dragging the wagon along the alley and toward the village center.

"Do you think he'll be okay?" Benjamin glanced at Charlie while they hurried past the closing stores. "I can't bear the thought of anything happening to Henry, especially at Christmas. The candle maker will be so upset."

Charlie nodded. "I think he'll pull through just fine. He's terribly thin and we'll have to pray that cut doesn't get infected, but I have a feeling the old man will take very good care of Henry."

Benjamin grinned. "I can't wait to see the candle maker's face."

Benjamin's stomach was full of knots and butterflies when they rounded the corner onto Main Street. There was a buzz of excitement in the air as neighbors exchanged Christmas greetings in passing, and several children raced around filled with boundless energy this night before Christmas.

"We're here then." Mr. Walker helped Jimmy with the wagon. "I think you should pull this up to the candle store, Ben. It looks like someone is waiting for you."

Benjamin took the rope from his father and gazed across the road. The candle maker stood at the door of his shop, the candle still glowing in the window. At that moment, a group of carolers started singing *Silent Night,* and the old man plodded down the steps, and onto the road.

"Henry? Have you come home, my boy? Where have you been?"

At the sound of his master's voice, Henry perked up in the wagon, and his whole body wiggled. Benjamin hurried across the street with the dog, followed by his brothers and father, all of them eager to see the reunion.

"Come here, my old Henry." The candle maker slowly bent over, tears streaming down his wrinkled face. Henry licked the old man's hand as if it was a lollipop, and Benjamin pumped a fist in the air.

"I knew it. I knew this was your dog. Merry Christmas, Mr. Candle Maker."

"Benjamin, I don't know how I'll ever thank you." The old man looked at the rest of the family. "Won't you all come in from the cold?"

"Thank you, sir. We will for a minute," Mr. Walker replied with a smile. "The rest of our family is waiting at home, so we won't stay long. Let Charlie and me carry old Henry inside."

Everyone shuffled into the cozy store and the candle maker fussed over the dog, making sure he drank and ate, and was perfectly comfortable on his blanket.

Charlie took one more look at Henry's leg in the light. "I'll pop by a couple more times this week to keep an eye on that cut. Other than that, give him plenty of water and feed him back up to his usual size. I think he's going to be good as new."

Benjamin's stomach clenched. He was going to have to leave Henry here. He rubbed the dog's ears and gave him a kiss on top of his velvety head.

"Wish I could take you home with me, boy," he whispered into the fur. "It's no wonder the old man was so upset at the thought of losing you."

"We should be going." Mr. Walker took Jimmy's hand. "My wife asked us to invite you over tomorrow for Christmas dinner, sir, unless you have other plans."

"Really?" The candle maker's eyes brightened. "That's very kind, I must say. I didn't have much planned at all, to be honest. I can bring over my plum pudding." He glanced at the dog and his shoulders sagged. "Second thoughts, I should stay home with poor old Henry. I couldn't leave him after all he's been through."

"We'll come and get him," Benjamin suggested. "Right, Father? I can bring one of my brothers and we'll wrap Henry up in the wagon and I'm sure we can get you a ride."

Mr. Walker laughed loudly. "Yes, yes. Your mother won't mind having a dog visit for Christmas Day."

"Thank you all so very much." The old man repeated his thanks over and over while they filed out the door onto the street. The carolers sang *Joy To The World*, and bells jingled in the night, while snow dusted their top hats and bonnets. Benjamin's heart felt like it might burst. He turned back to the candle maker.

"See you tomorrow, sir. I think this is going to be the best Christmas ever."

~ Ten ~

Benjamin patted his full stomach and sighed contentedly. He grinned from ear to ear when he looked around the crowded table. The room glowed in the warm light of Mother's red candle, and laughter filled the air. "This is the best Christmas ever."

"You say that every year," Charlie teased.

Mother interrupted. "Yes, but I think young Benjamin is right, and I'm enjoying every minute of it. This might be the last Christmas I have all my boys together to celebrate, especially now that Frank has asked his young lady to marry him."

Mr. Walker raised his glass and everyone toasted the newly engaged brother once more.

"It's certainly the best Christmas I've had in many years," the old candle maker agreed. "And I have you to thank for that, Benjamin."

Benjamin blushed. "I'm glad I found Henry, and I'm glad I found you, sir."

Jimmy held a yo-yo high in the air. "I think it's the best Christmas because I have a yo-yo of my very own, at long last."

Everyone laughed and Mrs. Walker disappeared into the kitchen to collect the plum pudding. She carefully carried it back to the table, and Jimmy cheered. "This is my favorite part of the whole meal, seeing who gets the slice of pudding with the six-pence inside."

"Be patient," Mrs. Walker scolded. "Nobody starts until we all have some pudding in front of us. And first, our dear friend wants to say something." She nodded at the candle maker.

The old man pushed back his chair and slowly stood. "I would like to thank you all, dear Walkers, for inviting me and old Henry to join in your Christmas. I'll never forget today. Secondly, I have a little something for you, Mrs. Walker." He delved into the satchel that hung on his chair, and pulled out a package tied with a yellow ribbon.

Mrs. Walker covered her face with her hands and gushed while she took the gift and held it to her chest.

"Open it, Mother," Benjamin urged.

40

"Yes, yes I will." With trembling hands, she untied the ribbon, folded back the paper, and gasped.

"Mother, you have a whole rainbow of candles." Jimmy whooped.

Mrs. Walker gazed from the beautiful selection of candles on her lap to the sweet old man standing next to her. With tears in her eyes, she managed to whisper, "Thank you, so very, very much."

The candle maker blew his nose with a large, white handkerchief. "You are most welcome, my dear. It's the least I could do. Now, before you boys start feasting on your pudding, there's something you should know."

"What's that?" Benjamin asked, spoon in hand.

"I have a special surprise for whoever has the slice with the sixpence inside."

"You mean, other than keeping the sixpence?" Jimmy asked.

"Oh, yes."

The room fell silent, apart from Henry snoring under the table.

Mr. Walker leaned over the table, picked up the lit red candle and held it above the pudding. The whole thing lit from the splash of brandy the candle maker brought along.

The boys clapped until the flames subsided, and then Mrs. Walker carefully dished out a slice for everyone.

"Go ahead then, it's time to eat up." She winked at the candle maker.

Spoons clattered and scraped the bowls, while the boys all carefully prodded the food before them.

"Here, I have it right here." Benjamin jumped up and held the pudding-covered coin above his head. "I won, I won."

His older brothers groaned, but Jimmy seemed as excited as Benjamin. "What's the surprise, what's the surprise?"

The candle maker reached back into his satchel and pulled out another parcel. "I suppose you should have this one then, Benjamin."

Benjamin gasped. Carefully, he slid the string from the

brown paper, savoring the moment. He only had one other pre-sent today, and even though he was very thankful, a new flat cap wasn't terribly exciting. This gift felt a lot more interesting.

"Come on, Ben, we haven't got all day." Charlie groaned.

"Okay, here goes." Benjamin ripped the paper aside, re-vealing a dark brown leather leash. "It's amazing." He sniffed the leather and pulled it out to its full length. He didn't wish to ap-pear ungrateful, but he was a little confused by the gift. "Thank you, I love it."

"What's it for?" Jimmy blurted out.

"Would you like to know, Benjamin?" The candle maker smiled. Benjamin nodded.

"I've spoken with your parents, and we have come to an agreement, which we think you'll be very happy with. I know you always wanted a dog of your own, and I understand that it's too much for your family to cope with at the moment. You know how much I love my Henry, and you also know that I'm not able to take him on walks anymore, which is maybe why he ran off and got lost last time. So we have a wonderful compromise—"

"Yes?" Benjamin could hardly breathe.

"You and I will jointly own Henry. I'll pay for his food and let him sleep at my place where there's lots of room, and you can walk him whenever you want, and bring him back here for visits and the like. Henry will get the best of both worlds. What do you think?"

Benjamin punched the air with his fist and let out a loud whoop. He dove under the table and tickled Henry's ears, and then rushed over to the candle maker and gave him a big hug.

"Thank you, Mister Candle Maker. Thank you for making me the happiest boy in the world, and for making this truly the very best Christmas ever. I'll take good care of Henry, I promise. And I'll never listen to rumors again, and I'll try to tame my own tongue. Oh, and I'll tell everyone that you sell the best sweets in the whole of England."

The candle maker chuckled and reached back into his satchel. "I almost forgot. Merry Christmas, Walker boys."

With a flourish, he emptied a bag full of peppermints, lemon

Sherbets, licorice, and toffees onto the table.

The boys cheered, grabbed a handful of goodies, and began to sing carols. Henry crawled out from under the table and curled up next to Benjamin, while the whole family joined in with a laughter-filled version of *Joy To The World*.

With a mouth full of toffee, Benjamin beamed. "I was right. It's the very best Christmas ever!"

~ End ~

Made in the USA
Charleston, SC
12 May 2016